The Haun
Hairy Surprise

There are more books about the Bailey City Monsters!

#1 The Monsters Next Door

#2 Howling at the Hauntlys'

#3 Vampire Trouble

#4 Kilmer's Pet Monster

The Hauntlys' Hairy Surprise

by **Marcia Thornton Jones**
and
Debbie Dadey

illustrated by **John Steven Gurney**

A
LITTLE APPLE
PAPERBACK

SCHOLASTIC INC.
New York   Toronto   London   Auckland   Sydney

For my husband, who can still surprise
me after fifteen years of marriage. And
to the great kids and teachers at
Braidwood Elementary in Braidwood,
Illinois — surprise! — DD

For Hannah and Brantley — May your lives
be filled with happy surprises! — MTJ

ISBN 0-590-04302-1

12 11 10 9 8 7 6 5 4 3 2 1   8 9/9 0 1 2 3/0

Printed in the U.S.A.   40

First Scholastic printing, September 1998

Contents

1.	Webbed Out	1
2.	A Hauntly Celebration	9
3.	Hauntly Creations	15
4.	Batty Time on Dedman Street	27
5.	Baseball, Nails, and Shopping	36
6.	Stranger than Strange	42
7.	Monster Express	48
8.	Kilmer's Surprise	56
9.	Monster Parade	67
10.	Monster Bash	75
11.	Monsters of Dedman Street	83
12.	Monster Madness	89
	Spooky Activities	96

1

Webbed Out

"What's wrong with Mrs. Hauntly?" Annie asked her older brother, Ben. Annie, Ben, and their neighbor Jane were on their way to school and had stopped by to pick up their friend Kilmer at Hauntly Manor Inn. They didn't see Kilmer, but they did see Kilmer's mother, Hilda Hauntly.

Hilda was sitting on the steps with her head down. Long, silky white cobwebs trailed off the porch railing onto Hilda's head, arms, and shoulders. In fact, spiderwebs practically covered Hilda, and a big black spider sat dangerously close to Hilda's head.

"Let's get the cobwebs off before that spider bites her," Jane suggested.

Ben shook his head. "No. That's one of

Kilmer's pet spiders," he said. "Minerva wouldn't hurt Mrs. Hauntly."

Annie knew about Kilmer's pet spiders, Minerva, Winifred, and Elvira, but she still wasn't used to seeing them. "Listen," Annie said, putting her finger to her lips. "I think Mrs. Hauntly is crying." Annie hurried up the sidewalk to the Hauntly Manor Inn porch. Jane and Ben followed her.

"Mrs. Hauntly," Annie asked, "are you all right?"

Hilda Hauntly looked up at Annie. Hilda's hair stuck up in all directions, with cobwebs laced throughout. Kilmer's spider Minerva was perched on the top of Hilda's mass of wild hair. Tears dripped down Hilda's chalk-white face. "Oh, I am so embarrassed," Hilda said in her unusual accent. "You caught me feeling sorry for myself."

"What's wrong?" Jane asked.

Hilda wiped a tear off her cheek, brushing a cobweb away from her face as she

did. "My birthday is this week," she admitted.

Jane nodded. "My mom always cries when it's her birthday. She hates getting old."

Hilda looked surprised. "I do not mind getting older. What bothers me is that I have never had a birthday away from my homeland. I miss Transylvania and the rest of my family and friends."

The door to Hauntly Manor Inn creaked open. Kilmer and his father, Boris Hauntly, swept out onto the porch. "My dear," Boris said, taking his wife's hand. "I had no idea you were so lonely for our homeland."

Hilda sighed. "Bailey City is very different from Transylvania," she admitted.

Annie looked at the Hauntly family. They were certainly different. Hilda's wild hair was strange enough, but she always wore a white lab coat covered with green, red, and purple stains. Boris Hauntly reminded Annie of a redheaded Count Dracula since he always wore a long black cape and had pointy teeth that were like fangs. Kilmer Hauntly had to be the most unusual fourth-grader Annie had ever seen. Even though he was in Ben and Jane's class, Kilmer was at least a head taller. Kilmer always managed to wear clothes that were too small and his hair was cut flat across his head just like the Frankenstein monster.

"Please forgive my foolishness," Hilda said. "You children run along to school. I will be fine."

Boris put a hand on Hilda's shoulder. "Have fun at school," Boris told the kids. "Please stop by after school for a treat."

Jane shuddered. Boris' treats were always something strange, like lizard lips or boiled buzzard eyeballs. "Let's get going," Jane said. "We don't want to be late." The four kids walked down Dedman Street toward the school.

Ben looked at his friend Kilmer. "You don't think your mother wants to move back to your old home, do you?"

"That would be terrible," Jane said. "We don't want you to move."

"We like having you as our neighbors," Annie added.

Kilmer shrugged. "She does like her job at F.A.T.S.," Kilmer said. F.A.T.S. stood for the Federal Aeronautics Technology Station where Hilda worked. "And my father loves running Hauntly Manor Inn. He enjoys all our guests."

Annie knew about the inn's guests. They always seemed to be the weirdest people. "But your mother is so homesick," Annie reminded Kilmer.

"You can't leave," Ben told Kilmer. "You're the only other boy on Dedman Street."

Jane laughed. "I'll make you a deal," she teased. "How about if you and Kilmer both move away and then there'll be no boys on Dedman Street?"

Ben held up a fist. "I'll make you a deal. How about I blast you into outer space and then there will be no dummies on Dedman Street?"

"Ha-ha," Jane said, looking both ways before crossing Forest Lane toward Bailey Elementary School. "You're so funny I forgot to laugh."

"Stop arguing," Annie told them. "This is serious. Dedman Street won't be the same if the Hauntlys leave."

"I know one thing," Ben said to Kilmer as they walked onto the school playground. "I'm going to do whatever it takes to keep you from moving. No matter what."

2

A Hauntly Celebration

At recess, Annie met her fourth-grade friends on the bleachers near the Bailey School soccer field. Kilmer sat with his head in his hands and sighed.

"Don't worry about your mother," Jane said, patting Kilmer on the back.

"My mother has never been this sad," Kilmer said. "It is very serious."

Annie snapped her fingers. "I've got the answer," she said.

"We're not worried about homework answers," Ben interrupted. "We need to help Kilmer and his mom."

Annie rolled her eyes. "I'm not talking about math problems. I've figured out a way to cheer up Mrs. Hauntly."

Kilmer sat up to look at Annie. "Do you mean it?" he asked.

"All she needs," Annie said, "is a birthday celebration!"

Kilmer thought for a moment. Then he sighed and slumped back down with his head in his hands.

"What's wrong?" Jane asked. "Annie's idea is perfect."

"No," Kilmer mumbled through his fingers. "It could never be the same here as it was back home."

"Sure it can," Ben said. "Tell us what you used to do at Castle Hauntly."

Kilmer sat up. He smiled and a faraway look came into his eyes as he remembered.

"The best parts of the Hauntly celebrations," Kilmer said, "were the feasts. Days before a party, the kitchen would warm up with all our favorite foods."

Annie grinned. "See," she said. "That's not different from our celebrations. Mom and Dad serve cookies and cakes and candy. What did they cook at Castle Hauntly?"

Kilmer licked his lips at the thought of his favorite treats. "I can almost smell the aroma drifting up from cauldrons full of my grandmother's gizzard goulash." Kilmer licked his lips again, and his stomach growled so loudly the bleachers shook.

Annie swallowed hard, and Jane's face turned as white as her sneakers. But Ben smiled with an evil grin. "I wonder if we could get that recipe to give our teachers for Christmas."

Kilmer shook his head. "The Bailey grocery store owner told my mother he doesn't carry specialty items and she'd have to fly back home if she wanted food like that."

"Oh, no," Jane said. "That was the worst thing he could have told your mother."

Annie nodded. "That's what probably made your mom start thinking about Castle Hauntly."

"Don't give up yet," Ben said. "I bet there's something we can do to make Mrs. Hauntly feel at home."

"For once Ben's right," Jane said. "Let's think some more. Didn't you have a birthday cake and candles at Castle Hauntly?"

Kilmer thought for a moment. "We didn't have candles, but torching was a great deal of fun."

Annie gulped before asking, "What is torching?"

Kilmer grinned. "We build a huge mountain of straw and wood, and with just a few torches we can have the entire mountain heated up by flames. Then we dance in the flickering shadows all night long."

Ben nodded. "I've heard of something like that before. They're called bonfires here, but we could never have one on Dedman Street. The Bailey City firefighters would have our bonfire put out before we could even roast a marshmallow."

"Besides," Jane added, "it would be very dangerous."

Kilmer sighed. "Just talking about it has made me understand why my mother is so sad," he said. "Maybe we should go back. I miss the dead trees on the mountain, the howling of night beasts, and the cold drafts of Castle Hauntly. It can never be the same on Dedman Street."

"Don't say that!" Ben told him. "It may not be exactly the same, but you can have fun in Bailey City, too."

"How?" Kilmer asked.

"W-Well," Ben stammered. "There's lots to do. We play soccer and baseball and football."

"But the best part," Annie said, "is that we do all those things with our friends. And you're our friend. If you left, then doing all those things wouldn't be as much fun!"

"You're right!" Kilmer said. He stomped his foot when he said it, and the entire bleachers shook again. "We would be very sad if we had to leave our new friends. It may not be the same as Castle Hauntly, but we can have fun right here on Dedman Street."

"Now," Jane said, "we just have to convince your mother."

"And that," Kilmer said, "will be the biggest problem of all."

3
Hauntly Creations

On Tuesday, Annie went straight home after school. She gathered a basket of thread, fabric, and buttons. Then she marched over to Hauntly Manor Inn. She stopped when she reached the front porch.

Hilda Hauntly sat on the steps. Kilmer's spider Minerva was busy spinning a web from Hilda's left ear to a nearby railing. Kilmer's other two spiders, Elvira and Winifred, worked together to drape a web from Hilda's shoulder all the way to the windowsill of Hauntly Manor Inn. Kilmer's spiders were famous for spinning webs. He had even studied their webs for his school science project.

"Good afternoon, Mrs. Hauntly," Annie said in her most cheerful voice. "Isn't it a beautiful day?"

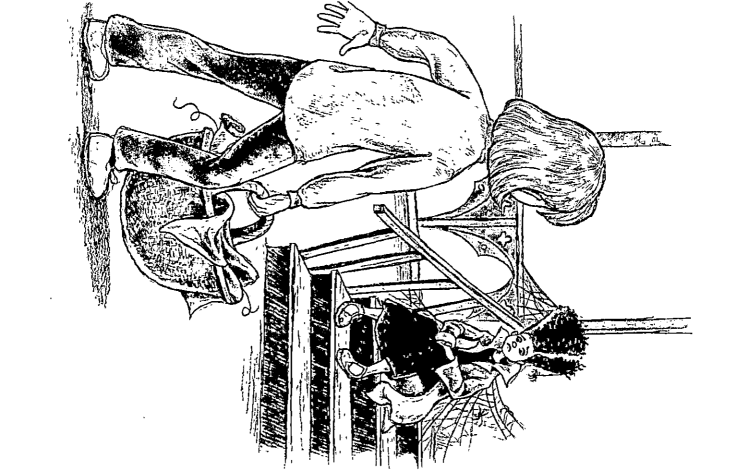

Hilda Hauntly sighed and looked at Annie with sad eyes. "It is very sunny today," Hilda said. "What a shame."

"But sunshine is good," Annie said. "It's just what we need."

Hilda looked confused. "I prefer the gray clouds."

"But," Annie told her, "we can see much better in the sunlight and I plan to teach you to sew."

"Sew?" Hilda said. "Why would I want to sew?"

"Sewing is a fun hobby," Annie told her. "You can create lots of neat things. It's just the thing to cheer you up."

Hilda shook her head. "I do not think I would be good at sewing. Besides, Kilmer's spiders are depending on me not to mess up their webs."

Annie looked at the intricate webs and realized Hilda had a point. If Hilda moved, the beautiful webs would be destroyed. Just then, Kilmer's black cat, Sparky, raced around the corner of Hauntly Manor Inn. As soon as she saw Annie, the cat skidded to a stop. Sparky's ears flattened against her head and she hissed. Her back arched up and her tail looked like it was alive with electricity. Annie didn't budge. She was used to the way Sparky flew around Hauntly Manor Inn as if fire-breathing dragons were trying to scorch her tail. Before Annie could stop her, Sparky darted up the steps, squeezed past Hilda, and landed right in the middle of Elvira's and Winifred's webs.

Sparky yowled. She turned three somer-saults. By the time she stopped to catch her breath, Sparky was completely covered with the sticky webs. Minerva, Elvira, and Winifred stopped spinning to see what their webs had caught. Then they chased Sparky off the end of the porch.

Annie laughed. "I never saw spiders chase a cat before," she told Hilda.

Hilda blinked away the tears in her eyes. "Elvira, Minerva, and Winifred are just little

babies," she said with a sniff. "I miss how the grown-up spiders chased us at Castle Hauntly."

Kilmer's spiders were the biggest, the hairiest, and the fastest spiders Annie had ever seen. She shivered at the idea of even bigger spiders.

"Well, Sparky has solved our sticky web problem," Annie said as she brushed the rest of the webs off Hilda. "Now we can get started on our sewing projects."

For the rest of the afternoon, Annie showed Hilda how to use patterns to cut fabric. She taught Hilda how to thread needles and how to stitch the pieces of material together. When Ben, Jane, and Kilmer came over to see how Hilda was doing, they were all surprised.

Jane smiled. "Let's see what you're making."

When Hilda held up the shirt she had made, nobody said a word. Instead, they stared at the four sleeves, all of them different lengths.

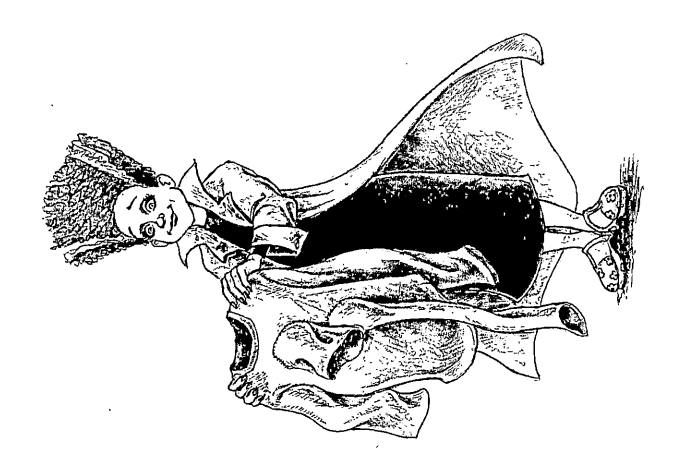

Ben finally broke the silence. "Is that a shirt for a horse?" he asked.

Hilda frowned. "Of course not. I made it for my cousin."

"Cousin Baxter will be very pleased," Kilmer told his mother.

"Show them what else you started," Annie said.

Hilda held up a jacket. It only had two sleeves, but one of them was five times longer than the other sleeve. "This is for my brother," she explained.

"Uncle Homer will be so happy," Kilmer said.

Ben didn't look so sure. "Maybe sewing isn't the best hobby for you," he said.

Hilda nodded. "Sewing is okay, but it makes me sad to make these creations for my family and friends. I will not get to see their faces when they open the packages."

"You're right," Jane said. "You need a hobby that makes you happy. And that gives me the perfect idea!"

On Wednesday, Jane told the rest of her

friends to meet her at the Hauntlys' front porch right after school. Just like the day before, Hilda sat on the porch, slumped against the railing.

Jane marched up the cracked sidewalk and set a big tape player on the porch. Music floated across the dried-up grass of the Hauntlys' front yard.

The door to Hauntly Manor Inn creaked open and Boris Hauntly peered down at them. "What is the music for?" he asked.

"We are going to teach Mrs. Hauntly to dance!" Jane said with a grin.

Boris smiled so wide the kids saw his pointy eyeteeth. "What fun. May Kilmer and I join you?"

"Of course!" Jane said. "We'll make it a party." Jane showed them all how to stand on their tippy toes and twirl like ballerinas.

Hilda, Boris, and even Kilmer stood on their toes. Then they started to spin. They spun and spun and spun until Annie, Ben, and Jane got dizzy from watching them. That's when the spinning Hauntlys collided and fell against a window, sending a crack all the way across it. Hilda held her hand to her head. "Dancing makes me dizzy," she said.

Jane put a different tape in the player. "Maybe ballet isn't the right kind of dance. Let's try tap dancing."

Jane pressed a button and fast music with lots of drumming blasted across Dedman Street. Jane showed the Hauntlys how to click their toes and heels on the porch to match the rhythm of the music.

Boris smiled. Hilda clapped. Kilmer jumped up. "Now, that looks like fun," Kilmer said.

Kilmer lifted one giant foot and started to tap. Only his taps sounded more like thumps. When Boris and Hilda joined him, the entire porch started shaking.

"Watch out!" Ben warned. But it was too late. The boards cracked and splintered, and then Boris, Hilda, and Kilmer disappeared from sight.

Jane, Annie, and Ben rushed over and

peered down the hole. "We are fine," Boris told them with a smile.

"But," Hilda said sadly, "I do not think dancing is the best hobby for us."

"Don't worry," Ben said. "I have the perfect idea!"

4

Batty Time on Dedman Street

On Thursday, Ben gathered Annie, Jane, and the Hauntlys in the backyard of Hauntly Manor Inn. "What we need," Ben told them, "is something we can do together. That's what makes baseball the perfect sport."

"Baseball?" Boris asked as he adjusted the black cape he always wore when he was outside. The flowing cape was fastened at his throat with a red button that looked exactly like a huge drop of blood. The cape made Boris look as if he had giant bat wings.

Annie nodded. "It's a fun game we can play."

"All you have to do," Jane added, "is hit

the ball with this Louisville Slugger." Jane picked up a baseball bat from the ground near Ben's feet.

"I like to slug things," Kilmer admitted. "What do we do after hitting the ball?"

"You run and touch each of the bases," Ben explained. "And when you go all the way around, it's called a home run."

Boris smiled. "That sounds like fun. I will go first."

Jane showed Boris how to swing at the ball. Then Ben threw a slow ball over home plate. Boris swung so hard he turned in a complete circle, but he missed the ball.

"Try again," Ben called. Then he pitched another ball.

This time, Boris hit the ball with a solid crack. "Run to the bases!" Annie yelled.

Boris ran so fast, the kids couldn't see his feet touch the ground. With his cape fluttering, he looked just like a giant vampire bat racing around the yard.

Jane clapped and Annie did a cheer. Ben

nodded at Boris. "You did great," he said. "Now let Kilmer try."

Kilmer stood at the base and waited for Ben to pitch the ball. Kilmer swung. CRACK! Kilmer hit the ball so hard it sailed way up over Ben's head, over the bushes, and out of sight.

"Wow," Ben yelled. "That's what I call a hit!"

"I am sorry I lost the ball," Kilmer said sadly.

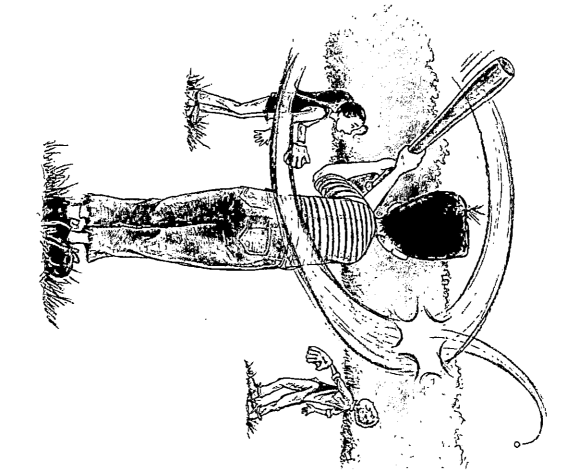

"Don't be sorry," Ben said with a grin. "I have another baseball. Besides, with a swing like that, you'll help the Bailey School baseball team to be champions this year."

"You mean I did well?" Kilmer asked.

Ben laughed. "You did great. Now it's your mom's turn."

Hilda walked up to home plate. "Here," Jane said. "Take the bat."

Hilda frowned and looked up in the air. "I see no bats."

"She didn't mean a flying bat," Annie said. "She's talking about the baseball bat."

Hilda shook her head. "I do not understand. Why do they call that stick a bat? It looks nothing like any bat I know."

Jane shrugged as she handed the bat to Hilda. "I don't know why they call it that."

Hilda held the bat. Then she shook her head again. "I cannot swing this thing called a bat," she said sadly. "It only makes me think of my family and friends at Castle Hauntly."

Hilda gently put the bat on the ground

and walked over to the back door, dragging her feet the entire way. As soon as she sat down on the step, Kilmer's spiders crawled out from a crack and started weaving a web around her ankles. Boris hurried over to Hilda and tried to cheer her up.

Ben, Jane, Annie, and Kilmer gathered under the branches of a dead maple tree. "This isn't working," Annie said. "We've only made Mrs. Hauntly sadder."

"And her birthday is only a few days away," Kilmer said.

"We have to think of something to make her birthday special," Ben said, "or else Mrs. Hauntly will want to move back to Castle Hauntly."

"I do not want to move away from my friends here on Dedman Street," Kilmer said. "How do you make your birthdays special?"

"That's easy," Jane said. "On my birthday, I get candy."

"Presents work for me," Ben said.

"I like opening packages wrapped in

bright paper and bows," Annie admitted. "But I like it even better when I have parties and all my friends and family come to see me."

"And then we light candles on top of a cake," Jane said. "The person having the birthday makes a wish and blows out the candles."

"Why do they want to put out the flames?" Kilmer asked.

"Because," Ben explained, "if you blow out all the candles with one big breath, they say your wish will come true."

"That's how we celebrate birthdays on Dedman Street," Annie said.

Kilmer looked at Ben, Jane, and Annie. "Friends, presents, candy. Magic candles and wishes coming true." Kilmer snapped his fingers. "You have just given me an idea," he said.

"What is it?" Annie asked.

Kilmer smiled and shook his head. "It will be a big surprise," he said. Then he ran across the yard and pulled Boris off to the

side. Annie, Jane, and Ben watched Kilmer whisper to Boris.

"What could Kilmer be planning?" Annie asked.

Ben shrugged. "I don't care, as long as it works."

"Knowing Kilmer," Jane said slowly, "it may be the biggest surprise ever on Dedman Street!"

5

Baseball, Nails, and Shopping

"Let's play baseball," Ben said to Kilmer after school the next day. "I brought a ball in my backpack."

Kilmer shook his head and continued walking across the school playground. A big group of kids, including Jane and Annie, was walking home as well. "I have to hurry to Hauntly Manor," Kilmer explained. "I have a lot to plan."

"What are you doing?" Jane asked.

Kilmer put his finger to his lips. "It is a secret surprise. Good-bye!" Kilmer waved and walked off the playground.

"I wish he'd let us help," Annie said.

Ben pulled out his ball and tossed it into the air. "I wish he'd play baseball," Ben said truthfully.

"He told Mr. Hauntly his idea," Annie reminded them. "We're his best friends. Why couldn't he tell us?"

Jane caught Ben's ball and laughed. "Maybe Mr. Hauntly is planning on turning everyone in Bailey City into vampires to make Mrs. Hauntly feel at home. After all, he sure looks like a vampire."

"Be quiet," Annie warned. "If someone hears you, they might think you're serious. The Hauntlys would be in big trouble."

Ben grabbed the ball from Jane. "We're the ones in trouble," Ben said. "We have to think of a way to make the Hauntlys like Bailey City more than Transylvania."

"Dedman Street sure would be boring if the Hauntlys moved away," Annie agreed.

"I know," Jane said. "I have a little money. We could buy Mrs. Hauntly a present. That way she'd be sure to like us."

Annie folded her arms in front of her chest. "You can't buy friendship," she said.

"You could buy mine," Ben said, "if you had enough money."

Annie watched Carey, a girl in third

37

grade, walk by. "You mean if Carey bought you a present you'd like her?" Annie whispered to Ben.

Ben's face turned red. "No way," he snapped. "I'd never like her."

"Maybe she can't help being the way she is," Annie said. "But you did just prove my point. You can't buy friendship."

"We can still show Mrs. Hauntly we like her," Jane said, pulling money out of her pocket. "I have one dollar and fifty cents. I could buy Mrs. Hauntly a birthday card. Maybe that will cheer her up."

"It couldn't hurt," Annie agreed. "I have a little money at home. We can get it, then walk down to Dover's department store to find a present."

"What about you?" Jane asked Ben. "Do you want to spend some money on her?"

Ben groaned and stuffed his baseball into his backpack. "I'd rather play baseball than shop. I'd rather eat nails than shop. But if it will help the Hauntlys stay in Bailey City, I'll do it."

The kids ran home, dropped off their backpacks, and grabbed nickels, dimes, and quarters from their banks. Fifteen minutes later they met in Dover's department store to look for a perfect gift for Hilda.

Ben held up a pair of green socks. "How about these?" he asked.

"Socks?" Annie said. "What kind of present is that?"

"Practical," Ben said. "Everybody needs them, and they keep your feet warm."

Jane rolled her eyes. "We should get something more exciting than that."

Ben pointed to the video games department. "That's where the exciting stuff is."

Annie shook her head. "We don't have enough money."

"We need something exciting and cheap," Ben said. "There is no such thing."

"Let's look at this book display," Jane suggested.

Ben gagged. "Books aren't exciting," he said. "Unless they have one about monsters."

Annie held up a book. It had been marked down to four dollars. The cover said *The Complete Haunted House Guide.* Annie read the back of the book: "This is the most comprehensive listing of haunted houses ever collected, complete with color photographs."

"That's creepy," Jane said, looking at the house on the front of the book. "It looks like something out of a horror movie."

Ben smiled. "It's perfect. Exciting, cheap — and scary. Perfect for a scary family like the Hauntlys."

"You shouldn't call them scary," Annie told her brother.

Ben shrugged. "Well, you have to admit the Hauntlys are a little bit different."

"Different?" came a screech from behind the three kids. "The Hauntlys are monsters! The Hauntlys should be run out of town!"

6

Stranger than Strange

Ben, Annie, and Jane stared at Carey. She kept talking about the Hauntlys.

"Kilmer is so weird, I'm surprised they let him go to Bailey Elementary," Carey told Ben. She used one hand to brush back a bunch of blonde curls. Her other hand held a huge clump of dresses to try on.

"You're the weird one if you think those dresses will make you look pretty," Ben teased. "Nothing will help you."

"Don't be mean," Annie told them both. "Everyone is different."

"My father said that the Hauntlys weren't quite right," Carey went on. "He said that there's something strange about them." Carey's dad was the president of the Bailey City Bank and Carey never let anyone forget it.

"You're not quite right, either," Jane pointed out. "And we let you stay around."

Carey tossed her dresses onto the book display. "I'm the normal one around here and Kilmer is some kind of . . . monster! He doesn't deserve to live in Bailey City."

Ben put his fist right up under Carey's nose. "You'd better take that back," Ben snarled at Carey.

Carey looked a little pale, but she didn't back down. "You wouldn't dare hit me," she said.

"Want to bet?" Ben asked, holding up his other fist.

"Wait a minute," Annie said, squeezing in front of Carey. "There's no reason to fight."

"Yes, there is," Jane said. "Did you hear what she said about Kilmer?"

"Sticks and stones can break my bones, but names can never hurt me," Annie reminded her.

Ben tried to pull Annie out of the way. "I'm going to be breaking bones in a minute if you'll move," he said.

43

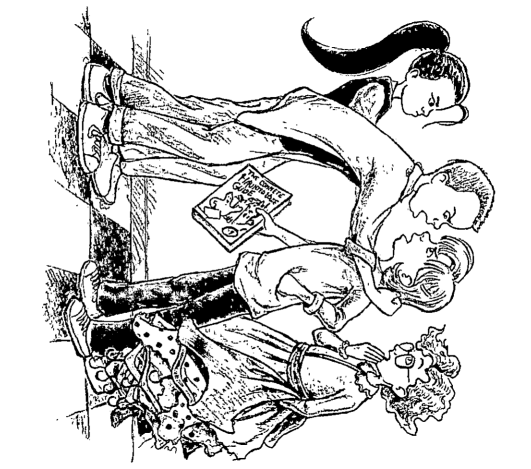

Annie stood her ground with Carey trembling behind her. "If you want to hurt her, you'll have to go through me," Annie said.

"How can you defend her?" Jane asked. "She just said horrible things about Kilmer."

Annie nodded. "I know she's a jerk."

"I am not," Carey interrupted.

"But violence never solved anything," Annie continued.

"It would make me feel better," Ben said.

Annie held up the haunted house book. "Why don't we just buy this and take it to Kilmer's?"

"I'll make you a deal," Jane told Carey. "You promise never to say anything bad about Kilmer and we'll pretend this whole thing never happened."

Carey didn't give up that easily. "I'll make you a deal. I'll go with you to Kilmer's house and prove he is stranger than strange."

"Fine," Ben snapped, looking Carey straight in the eye.

"Fine," Carey said. She snapped her fingers at a nearby salesclerk. "Put these on my daddy's account," Carey said. "He'll pick them up later."

Annie gulped. There had to be at least ten dresses in that pile, and the dresses at Dover's were not cheap. The four kids didn't say a word as Jane used all the money they had collected to pay for the book. Then they walked down Forest Lane to Dedman Street.

There was a chill in the air and Jane pulled her sweater around her. The wind howled as they got closer to Thirteen Dedman Street, but that wasn't unusual. The wind always blew more at the Hauntlys'.

"This place looks haunted," Carey pointed out as they stood beside Hauntly Manor Inn.

Jane thought the same thing, but she wasn't about to admit it to Carey. "It just needs a coat of paint," Jane said. All of the kids knew that Hauntly Manor needed more than paint. Even though it was less than a year old, most of the windows were cracked and the porch sagged in the middle. Kilmer's black cat hissed at them from beside a dead bush. Huge cobwebs covered every inch of the doorway, and the grass in the yard crunched dead under their feet. A rusty sign swung in the moaning wind. The sign said HAUNTLY MANOR INN.

"I think the health department should condemn the inn," Carey said matter-of-factly. "I'll tell my father to see to it."

"No!" Annie yelled. "You can't do that."

Carey lifted her nose in the air. "I can do anything I want."

"But don't you want to have friends?" Annie asked.

Carey didn't answer Annie. Carey was looking at something rolling down Dedman Street. "Oh, my gosh," she said. "Take a look at what those crazy Hauntlys are doing now!"

7

Monster Express

A huge black truck rolled up in front of Hauntly Manor. Then another and another. The four kids backed down the sidewalk and hid from view behind the bushes in Ben's yard to watch the three trucks.

"What's going on?" Annie asked.

"Oh, no!" Ben moaned. "The Hauntlys are moving after all."

Jane held up the book. "I guess we wasted our money."

"Now it will be a going-away present," Annie said sadly.

"I don't think they're going anywhere," Carey pointed out. "They're carrying stuff in — not out." Big, muscular moving men and women lifted huge boxes off the trucks. The boxes were long and wooden. Instead of carrying them in the front door, the movers took them around to the conservatory. Ben, Annie, and Jane knew the conservatory was a big glass room at the back of Hauntly Manor. Boris Hauntly kept his dead plants in there.

"What is all that stuff they're unloading?" Annie wondered out loud.

"Probably monster parts," Carey said matter-of-factly. "Or dead bodies."

Ben held up his fist. "You'd better quit saying mean things about the Hauntlys," he warned. He might say mean things, but he sure didn't want Carey saying them, especially about the Hauntlys.

"Look!" Jane said, interrupting Ben. "Here comes another truck."

"It looks more like a bus to me," Annie told her friends. "It's not a Bailey City bus, though." Bailey City buses were bright blue with red writing on the sides. This bus was blacker than midnight with strange purple writing on the side.

"What does it say?" Carey asked, straining to read the strange scrawl.

The bus screeched to a stop and black smoke filled the air around it. In a few moments, the smoke cleared. The bus stood behind the moving vans, almost right in front of the kids. They each read the purple words on the side of the bus out loud: "Monster Express."

"Monster Express!" Carey squealed. "I told you those Hauntlys are nothing but monsters. This proves it!"

Ben gulped, but he quickly defended the Hauntlys. "That doesn't prove anything.

Lots of things are named after monsters."

"That's right," Annie agreed. "It doesn't mean they're real."

"They look awfully real to me," Carey said, pointing to the people stepping off the bus. "And hairy."

The four kids crouched down and stared at the strangers climbing off the Monster Express. The first creature was so tall she had to stoop to get down. She was pale, paler than a sheet of white paper. That wasn't so strange, but when she pulled

back her white hood, the kids saw that even her hair was almost colorless. The only thing that had any color were her eyes. They were green like slime, and they glowed in the daylight. Annie shivered when the strange lady looked their way.

The strange lady glided across the dead grass, following the movers to the conservatory. The next person to step off the bus didn't look like a person at all. He looked more like a big dog, or wolf. Hair covered every inch of his body.

"That's the hairiest person I've ever seen," Carey whispered.

"Maybe he's Fang's dad," Jane said. Fang was Kilmer's cousin. He had visited for a while and, although he was only a teenager, he could have easily won a hairiest man contest.

"Then that must be the Creature from the Black Lagoon's sister," Ben joked, but he was partly serious. The next person to step off the bus had bright green hair and bright green clothes and even bright green

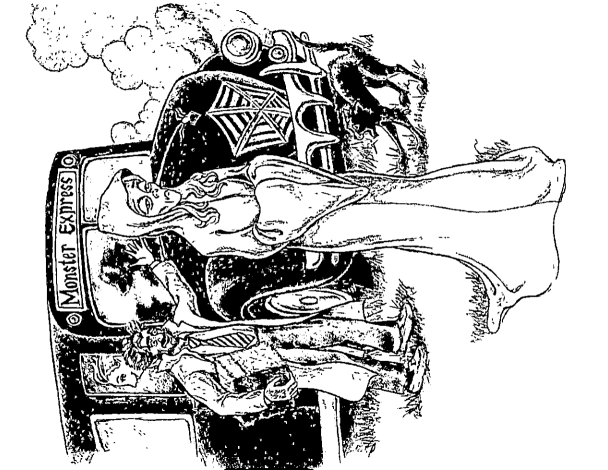

fingernails. Jane had to admit the lady's long nose, pointy ears, and strange clothes made her look like something straight from the Black Lagoon.

"I know her," Annie said softly when the next person descended from the bus. "That's Priscilla Pocus. She has been a guest at the inn before." Priscilla Pocus was the guest who'd said strange rhymes that seemed to be magical.

"I'm going to tell her hello," Annie said, starting to stand up.

"No," Jane said, grabbing her. "Look!"

A cold wind blew violently through the bushes as the next guest swept off the bus. She was dressed in black, just like Priscilla Pocus. The new lady cackled an evil laugh and her bony hand held out a long, ancient stick. She pointed the broom right at the kids.

"She knows we're here," Carey whimpered.

"So what?" Ben said. "It's my yard."

"I don't care," Jane said with a gulp. "There's something scary about that lady. I'm getting out of here."

Jane, Carey, Annie, and Ben all stood up to run away, but they didn't get the chance.

8

Kilmer's Surprise

Boris and Kilmer suddenly appeared behind them.

Ben, Jane, and Annie were so surprised, they couldn't move. Carey took one look at Boris' pointy eyeteeth and screamed. Before anyone could stop her, Carey sprinted down Dedman Street, screaming the entire way.

"Humph," Boris said with his hand on Kilmer's shoulder. "That girl is behaving very strangely."

Kilmer nodded. "She acts like that every time I see her."

Boris shivered and adjusted the long black cape slung over his shoulders. "All that bouncy yellow hair," Boris said, "and

those huge blue eyes are enough to scare a person."

Ben laughed. "I agree. Carey *is* the scariest person in Bailey City."

"Ben is right about that," Jane said. "We should all watch out for Carey and her father. They can cause big problems."

Kilmer shrugged his huge shoulders. "We do not have time to worry about Carey. We have bigger problems."

"Kilmer says you will help," Boris added, "because you are our friends."

Annie nodded. "How can we help?" she asked.

"Come inside," Boris said. "And we will tell you about it." Then Boris turned and glided toward the door to the conservatory. Kilmer trudged along behind him.

"Do you think it's safe to go in there with all those creepy people?" Annie asked Jane and Ben.

"We have to go," Ben said. "Helping the Hauntlys might convince them to stay."

"The Hauntlys won't let anything happen to us," Jane added, but she didn't sound very sure.

Together, the three kids followed Boris and Kilmer around the side of Hauntly Manor Inn toward the glassed-in conservatory. When the Hauntlys first moved in, the glass room was bright and cheerful, the perfect place for growing colorful flowers and green vines. But now the windows were streaked with grime and four cracks zigzagged across the glass like huge jagged scars.

The first thing the kids noticed when they followed Boris and Kilmer into the conservatory was a strong smell. They knew it wasn't Boris' plants. Hundreds of clay pots lined the glass walls, but they were all filled with dried-up twigs. Only one plant looked as if it was still alive. It was gigantic, reaching at least seven feet into the air. Annie thought it watched her every move, waiting for her to get close enough

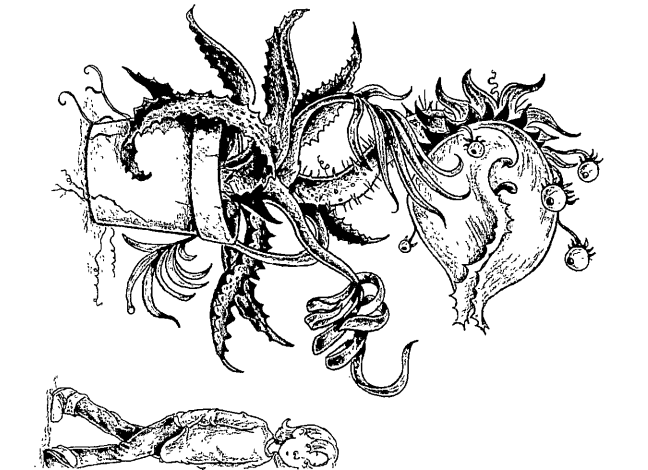

so it could bite her. She walked as far away from it as she could.

All the visitors who had climbed off the Monster Express were perched on dirt piled in four long flower beds in the center of the conservatory. Sparky, Kilmer's cat, was digging in one of the dirt-filled boxes. It looked as if she was trying to bury something. Annie tried not to think about what might be under the mound of rich black soil.

Boris held out his arms to the strangers in the conservatory. "I would like to introduce you to our big surprise," he said with a smile so wide his pointy eyeteeth showed. "These are our dearest friends from Transylvania."

"That's Uncle Barker," Kilmer said, pointing to the man covered with hair. Uncle Barker leaned against a huge box that was covered with green, hairy mold. He scratched behind his ear and sniffed at the kids.

.

"And you know Priscilla," Boris said. Priscilla waved at them.

"Sirena is a family friend. She has a captivating singing voice," Boris said. The lady with bright green hair was too busy grabbing at something in a bucket of muddy water to notice the kids.

"Kay Davver is my second cousin, once removed," Kilmer said. The tall lady with long white hair glared at them with her slime-green eyes.

"And this is Hex, our very old friend," Boris said, pointing to the woman with the ancient stick. "She'll be picking up the rest of our friends."

"I saw you," she said in a voice so screechy it sounded like fingernails scratching a chalkboard. "You spied on us from the bushes next door."

"We're s-s-sorry," Annie stammered.

"We didn't mean to be rude," Jane added.

Kilmer grinned at the unusual group of people. "They came all this way just for Mother's surprise birthday party."

62

"Party?" Annie, Jane, and Ben said at once.

Kilmer nodded. "When you told me about your celebrations, it gave me this wonderful idea. We invited all our relatives and friends to Hauntly Manor Inn."

"The only problem is," Boris said, "we must hide our surprise visitors from Hilda. Or her birthday surprise will be ruined."

"Hiding is going to be hard," Ben mumbled as he sniffed the air. "That smell is

strong enough to alert the Bailey City garbage dump."

Uncle Barker growled and patted the moldy box. "You must be talking about our surprise treat," he said in a voice so low and rough it sounded like tree bark.

"And we don't want Mother to see it until the party begins after sundown," Kilmer explained. "That's why we need your help. Mother may come home from work any minute."

"How can we help?" Annie asked.

"We need you to hide our visitors," Boris told them.

"And my box," Uncle Barker added.

"Until the party starts," Kilmer finished.

"Will you do it?" Boris asked.

Ben looked at Annie. Annie looked at Jane. Jane took a deep breath and spoke for them all. "Of course," she said.

"I just have one question," Ben said to Kilmer. "Where do you plan to have this big party?"

Kilmer smiled. "That's the best part. We are having it out front so the entire neighborhood can join us! Isn't that a great idea?"

"One thing is certain," Jane said with a gulp. "Mrs. Hauntly will be surprised. Very surprised."

"And that's not all," Annie added. "So will the rest of Dedman Street!"

9
Monster Parade

Ben led the way out the conservatory door into the Hauntlys' backyard. Jane and Annie followed close behind him. After them came Kilmer's Transylvanian friends and relatives. They looked like a monster parade. Hex waved and got into the Monster Express bus.

"What will the neighbors think?" Jane whispered to Ben and Annie.

"They won't think anything because they aren't going to know," Ben hissed. He disappeared through a gap in the hedges that separated the Hauntlys' yard from Ben and Annie's backyard.

"We have to hide them from more than just Mrs. Hauntly," Annie told Jane once they had pushed through the hedges. "We have to hide them from everyone."

"Especially Carey," Ben added.

"How do you suggest we hide a witch, zombie, werewolf, and swamp monster?" Jane whispered to Annie and Ben as they waited for the Hauntly visitors to make their way into Ben and Annie's backyard. "After all, your house doesn't have any secret passageways or a single trapdoor!"

"We could hide them under the beds and in the closets," Annie suggested.

"That's a stupid idea," Ben told her. "Everyone knows those are the first places to check for monsters."

"We have to think of something," Annie said. "We can't just let a group of monsters hang out in our backyard."

The three kids glanced at Kilmer's guests. Priscilla was talking to her broomstick. Kay Davver stood in the middle of the yard, staring at absolutely nothing. Sirena picked up a stick and tossed it across the yard. When she did, Uncle Barker dropped the fuzzy box and chased the stick. He grabbed the stick and raced back to Sirena. Uncle Barker held his nose high in the air and sniffed.

"I smell trouble," Uncle Barker growled. "Somebody is coming."

"I don't see how he can smell anything with that stinking box so close," Jane grumbled.

"That box is the least of our troubles," Ben said. "Quick, get them inside."

Jane, Ben, and Annie rushed the Hauntly visitors into their house. Everybody but Uncle Barker, that is.

"I prefer to stay outside," he growled at Ben.

"But you have to hide," Ben told him.

Uncle Barker licked his lips and scratched behind his ear. "Don't worry about me," he said. "I'll find a nice shady spot for a nap." He trotted across the yard to disappear into the shadows of a weeping willow tree.

Ben didn't have time to argue so he let

Uncle Barker go. Ben hurried inside and found everybody else gathered in the den.

"Why are you standing around?" Ben snapped to Annie and Jane. "Shouldn't we hide everybody before Mrs. Hauntly sees them?"

"We'll be fine," Jane said, "as long as we keep them out of sight." Jane quickly shut the heavy curtains in the den, blocking out the sunshine.

"Thank you," Kay Davver whispered. "I think I will take a little nap." She lay down on the couch, but she quickly sat up. "It is not dark enough for me to rest. Do you have a blanket so I can cover my eyes?"

Annie handed Kay a blanket. Kay completely covered her body with the blanket and settled down for a nap.

"Water?" Sirena said softly as she tapped Ben on the shoulder. "May I have water?"

"Me, too," Priscilla said.

Ben pointed toward the bathroom. "There are cups in there. Help yourself."

Just then the doorbell rang. Everybody froze. "Now what?" Annie gulped.

"Don't give up so easily," Ben said with a grin. "We're pretty good at getting out of trouble."

"I've got it!" Annie said. "You take care of whoever it is. Don't invite them in!"

When the doorbell rang again, Ben and Jane hurried to open the front door. "What are YOU doing here?" Ben muttered.

Carey batted her long eyelashes at him and pushed back a handful of blonde curls. "I have come to tell you, you're not going to get away with this."

"Get away with what?" Jane asked.

Carey pointed a finger at Ben's nose. "I know you're helping the Hauntlys and all the freaky people who climbed off the Monster Express. I'm going to stop you and the rest of those monsters from invading Bailey City."

Ben rolled his eyes. "Aren't you a little old to believe in fairy-tale monsters?" he asked.

"This is not a fairy tale," Carey said. "I know you're hiding the Hauntly monsters in your house."

"The only monster in here," Annie said as she came to the door, "is Ben."

"If that's true," Carey said, "then you'll let me come inside." Before anybody could stop her, Carey pushed Ben aside and stomped into the den. Then she tramped down the hall. Annie, Ben, and Jane

followed Carey as she marched all over the house.

Carey stopped just outside the bathroom door. Splashing sounds came from inside. "Who's in there?" Carey demanded.

"Just a relative," Ben said with a smile.

When the kids were near the front door again, Carey stopped and glared at the three friends. "I don't know where you hid them," Carey said, "but I know they're here someplace. I'm telling my father, and he'll be sure to find them. When he does, you'll be sorry!"

10

Monster Bash

"Carey's going to cause the Hauntlys big trouble," Annie said.

Ben slammed the door shut. "I'm not worried about that little snitch."

"I'll get Sirena and Priscilla," Annie said, going down the hall. "Don't forget to uncover Kay Davver before she wakes up."

"She gives me the creeps. She looks like a dead body under there," Ben said.

Annie giggled nervously. "Like a real cadaver."

Just then a loud knocking rattled the back door. They all froze.

"She's baaaaaaaack," Annie whispered.

"We have to hide them again," Jane gulped.

"No," Ben said firmly. "We don't have time. Besides, I've had enough of Carey pushing us around. I'm going to get rid of her once and for all."

Before they could stop him, Ben rushed to the door and pulled it open. But it wasn't Carey they found standing at the door.

"Good evening," Boris said, smiling and showing his pointy eyeteeth. "The time has arrived. Follow me to the party."

Ben, Annie, Jane, Kay Davver, Sirena, Priscilla, and Boris made an unusual parade across the backyard. Uncle Barker slipped from the shadows to join them as they made their way over to the inn. What they saw amazed even Ben.

The entire front yard of Hauntly Manor had been transformed. Huge candelabras cast eerie shadows as hundreds of black balloons danced over food-laden tables.

In front of Hauntly Manor Inn, the Monster Express roared to a stop. Black smoke enveloped the entire bus for a moment before clearing. The doors creaked open and more strange visitors appeared. Boris

greeted the new guests and led them to the center of the decorated yard.

Kilmer clomped over to his friends. "The party is almost ready to begin," he said with a big smile. "We are waiting for Mother."

"Please have some refreshments," Boris said as he glided up behind Kilmer. The kids stared at the food as Boris pointed out weird-looking delicacies. "Please help yourselves," he said.

Jane gulped. "We'll just wait for the birthday cake."

Boris smiled and waved his hand. "It is lovely. I made it myself!" The kids admired the huge five-layer birthday cake. It was big and it was black. Even the birthday candles were black. Little skeletons danced all around the edge of the cake.

"It looks great," Annie said to be polite.

Just then the Hauntlys' black station wagon stopped in front of Hauntly Manor. Hilda stepped out and everyone yelled, "Surprise!"

Hilda took one look and started bawling.

"Oh, no," Ben said as Hilda sobbed. "She hates it."

Annie had to admit that Ben was right. "I guess inviting all these people was a big mistake."

"Now the Hauntlys will move for sure," Jane agreed.

"We have to do something," Annie said miserably.

Ben's face lit up like the skeleton cake. "I have an idea. Follow me." Ben raced to his house with Annie and Jane. Fifteen minutes later Ben came out of his house looking totally different. He had a black, curly wig on his head and brown patches of hair glued all over his face, fingers, and arms.

Annie giggled. "You look like a rat that got in a fight with a tiger."

"I don't care what it looks like as long as this plan works," Ben told her. "Are you guys ready?"

Annie stuffed a pillow into the shirt Hilda had made. "Do I make a good Hunchback of Notre Dame?" she asked.

"What do you think of my four arms?" Jane asked, twirling around in the four-armed shirt that Hilda had made.

Ben howled his approval and patted the stack of invitations he had printed out on his dad's computer. "Let's hurry before the Hauntlys decide to go back to Transylvania on the Monster Express."

"Maybe if the Hauntlys see everyone on our street dressed up like their friends and relatives they will want to stay here," Annie said, leaning over so her hump would stick up better.

Ben, Annie, and Jane went to every house on Dedman Street. They knocked on doors and rang doorbells. Every person got one of the invitations that read:

HAUNTED PARTY
Dress-Up Like a
MOVIE MONSTER
and HAVE FUN!
at the HAUNTLY MANOR INN
COME NOW!

"Do you really think this will work?" Annie asked.

"If it doesn't," Jane said, "then we can kiss the Hauntlys good-bye."

Ben shuddered. "I'm not kissing anyone."

"Come on," Annie said, "let's surprise Mrs. Hauntly."

Ben, Annie, and Jane rushed down Dedman Street to Hauntly Manor Inn. They raced up to Hilda and shouted, "Surprise!"

Hilda looked at Ben, Annie, and Jane. She didn't say a word. In fact, a deadly hush came over the entire party. No one said a word. Everyone just stared at the three kids.

11
Monsters of Dedman Street

Ben, Annie, and Jane were completely surrounded by the Hauntlys' Transylvanian friends. Kay Davver poked the hump on Annie's back. Uncle Barker sniffed at the fake fur glued to Ben's fingers. Priscilla Pocus stared at the four arms dangling from Jane's shirt.

Priscilla pointed a crooked finger at the three children and stepped even closer. "Here are three monsters that are new to me. Who are these strangers I suddenly see?" Priscilla asked.

Ben held up his hand before she got any closer. "We're not strangers," he said. "It's just us."

Jane nodded. "Don't you recognize us?"

Boris, Hilda, and Kilmer pushed their way through the crowd. Hilda wiped the

tears from her face and bent down to get a closer look at the kids. "Is that Ben, Annie, and Jane?" she asked.

Annie smiled through her disguise and nodded so hard, the hump on her back slipped down. "We dressed up for your party," she explained.

"That way you'll feel like this is your home," Jane added.

"And you'll like us," Ben added.

Hilda's forehead wrinkled in a frown as she thought about what the kids had said. "I can understand why you would want to look this way," Hilda finally said. "But I liked you just the way you were."

"But we don't want you to leave Dedman Street," Annie said.

"Why would we leave?" Boris asked.

"Because you're homesick," Jane said sadly.

"It is true I miss Transylvania and all my friends," Hilda said loudly enough so everyone could hear, "but I do not want to leave Bailey City."

"You don't?" Ben asked hopefully.

Hilda smiled. "Dedman Street is an exciting place for us to live," she explained. "It is such an unusual place. We never know what surprises are in store for us."

Just then, doors from nearby houses swung open. The Hauntlys' visitors stepped back into the shadows as neighbors streamed from their houses. Everybody laughed, even Hilda, when they saw that all the neighbors were dressed up.

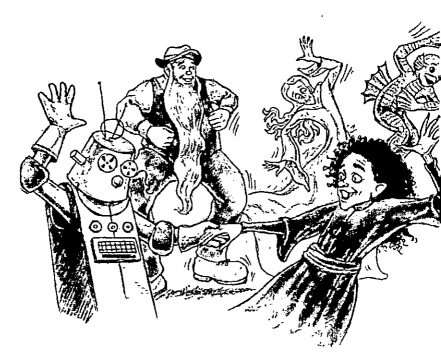

There was a mummy, a robot, and even a swamp monster.

Ben grinned. "We invited some neighbors to your party," Ben said. "And they dressed up just for you!"

"What a lovely surprise!" Hilda said.

Boris greeted all the guests and Kilmer hurried to put on some music. Jane showed them all her dance steps, and soon it was hard to tell the real monsters from the neighbors as they danced on the Hauntlys'

dead lawn. Everybody laughed when Ben and Uncle Barker had a howling contest. They were having a great time, especially Hilda.

"Everything is going great," Jane told Ben and Annie.

"I think we've convinced the Hauntlys to stay in Bailey City!" Annie said.

"Our troubles are over," Ben said. "Thanks to me and my monster idea."

Just then, a black limousine turned the corner and raced down Dedman Street. When it screeched to a stop right in front of the inn, the Hauntlys' guests scooted back into the shadows. Ben darted into the shadows, too. The neighbors dressed as monsters were left standing in the middle of the yard.

Two limousine doors swung open. Annie gasped. Jane just shook her head.

"Our troubles aren't over, after all," Jane said sadly. "It looks as if they've just begun!"

12

Monster Madness

Carey and her father stood by the long, shiny limousine, and they didn't look happy.

"I told you they were monsters," Carey told her father loudly enough so everyone could hear. "You have to make them leave Bailey City at once!"

Carey and her father marched up the cracked sidewalk and stopped right in front of Hilda, Boris, and Kilmer. "What is the meaning of this monster madness?" Carey's father asked Boris.

Boris didn't have a chance to answer because just then, something tapped Carey on the shoulder. Carey looked down at a very hairy finger on her shoulder. "AAAAAH-HHHHH!" she screamed at the top of her lungs. Carey tore off down the cracked sidewalk, screaming all the way.

Everybody stared at her until she disappeared around a corner. Then they looked down at the hairy monster that had scared her away. There stood Ben, grinning up at the entire group.

"Gee," Ben said. "I wanted to scare her, but I didn't mean to do such a good job."

Kilmer laughed. "It is easy to scare Carey," he said. "I just have to look at her and she gets scared."

Hilda and Boris laughed. So did Carey's father. "Carey didn't understand this was a costume party," Carey's father said. "I guess she jumped to conclusions. We're sorry we bothered you."

Boris smiled so wide, moonlight glinted off his eyeteeth. "It was no bother," Boris said. "Perhaps she is only upset that we did not invite her to Hilda's birthday party. You are both welcome to stay."

Carey's father shook Hilda's hand, wished her a happy birthday, and then he

drove away in his limousine to look for Carey. As soon as he was gone, Kay Davver turned up the music and the rest of the Hauntlys' visitors emerged from the shadows and started dancing. Uncle Barker carried the mysterious fuzzy box and placed it in front of Hilda.

"What is this?" Hilda asked.

"We brought birthday treats all the way from Transylvania," Uncle Barker told her. "Happy birthday!"

Boris and Kilmer helped Hilda crack

open the lid. A powerful aroma nearly knocked Ben, Jane, and Annie over. They held their noses and stepped closer to peer inside. Black piles of fish eggs and gooey blobs were packed inside.

"All my favorites!" Hilda said. She immediately reached into the box and slurped up fish eggs.

"All these surprises have been wonderful," Hilda told Boris and Kilmer.

"You have Ben, Jane, and Annie to thank," Kilmer explained. "They told us all about surprise parties and birthday presents."

"That reminds me," Jane said, pulling out a gift from her costume. "We brought you a present, too."

Hilda tore open the paper and gasped when she saw *The Complete Haunted House Guide*. "Look!" she said with a laugh. "There's Aunt Lulu's house. And that's Cousin Griswald's summer cottage." Hilda hugged Ben, Annie, and Jane. "You are the best neighbors in the entire world," she told them.

Boris nodded. "You proved to us that this is our home now," he said.

"We would not dream of moving from Dedman Street and our new best friends," Hilda said.

Ben, Jane, and Annie cheered. Kilmer jumped up. When he landed, a new crack zigzagged across the sidewalk.

Hilda didn't look sad anymore. She looked very happy. "This has been the best party ever," she said.

"It is not over yet," Boris said as he grabbed Hilda's hand and led her to the nearby table. Every candle glowed on her five-layer black birthday cake. Shadows flickered across Hilda's face and Ben, Annie, and Jane sang "Happy Birthday."

"Make a wish and blow out all the candles!" Annie said.

Hilda closed her eyes and concentrated on her wish. Then she blew out every single candle on the cake. The crowd cheered.

"What did you wish for?" Ben asked.

"I wished," Hilda said, "that we could have surprise parties every single year!"

Boris scratched his chin. "But if we plan the parties now, they won't be a surprise."

Ben shook his head. "Don't worry. I think Hilda's wish will come true," Ben told the Hauntlys, "because you never know when to expect surprises on Dedman Street!"

Spooky Activities

Hauntly Word Search

Find the words in the spooky web below. Words can be horizontal, vertical, diagonal, and even backward!

HILDA ✳ SPARKY
BORIS ✳ HAUNTLY MANOR
KILMER ✳ DEDMAN ST
MONSTER BASH ✳ HAIRY
SURPRISE ✳ BIRTHDAY

```
H  A  D  E  D  M  A  N  S  T  R
M  O  N  Y  S  P  A  R  K  Y  O
B  O  T  H  D  A  L  H  B  J  N
I  Y  N  R  B  Y  B  A  O  T  A
R  B  T  S  E  N  R  I  R  D  M
T  E  M  E  T  M  O  R  I  S  Y
H  S  A  B  I  E  L  Y  S  M  L
D  I  P  R  D  Y  R  I  H  E  T
A  R  H  I  L  D  A  B  K  P  N
Y  P  I  S  E  L  K  S  A  N  U
S  U  R  P  R  I  S  E  B  S  A
S  T  E  R  T  H  D  A  R  E  H
```

Answer page 106

Yummy Good-Looking Eyeballs

You will need:
small powdered-sugar doughnut holes
Lifesaver candies
chocolate chips
red decorating gel

Carefully put decorating gel on a piece of candy and place on the doughnut hole. Take a chocolate chip, put a little decorating gel on the tip, and press it into the center of the candy's hole. Make a few red squiggly lines on the doughnut hole with the gel. It's an eyeball that is good-looking and delicious to eat!

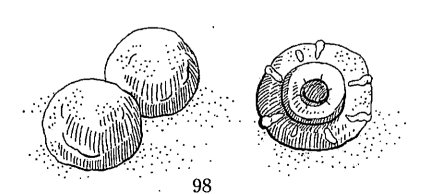

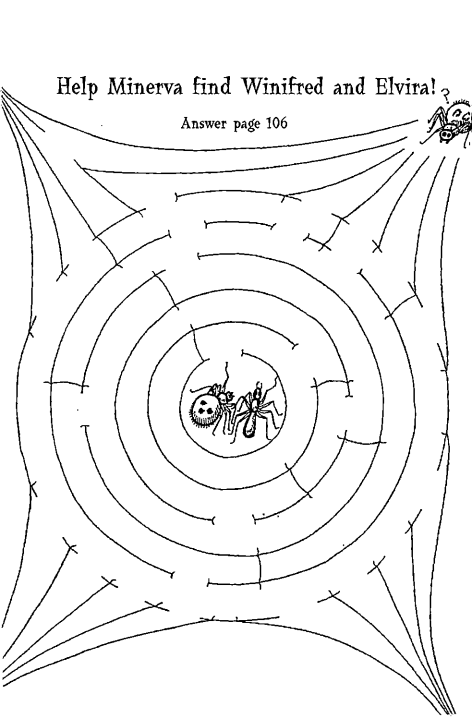

Help Minerva find Winifred and Elvira!

Answer page 106

Spooky Graveyard Brownies

You will need: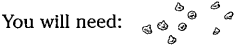

1 package of brownie mix, plus the ingredients listed on the box
5 to 7 long rectangular cookies (such as chocolate-covered graham crackers)
4 to 7 marshmallows
⅛ cup semi-sweet chocolate chips
4 to 6 round orange jellied candies
4 to 7 animal-shaped cookies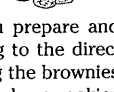

Ask a grown-up to help you prepare and bake the brownies according to the directions on the box. After taking the brownies out of the oven, press in the long cookies so some are standing straight and some are leaning. These are the tombstones! While the brownies cool, use your imagination to decorate your graveyard scene. Here are some suggestions:
* To make a ghost, gently twist the top of a

marshmallow into a point and stick a tooth-pick inside it. Ask a grown-up to melt the chocolate chips. Then dip a toothpick into the chocolate and draw a face on the marshmallow. Add as many ghosts as you want to the graveyard!

* To make a jack-o'-lantern, use either mini sugar pumpkins or round orange jellied candies. Dip another toothpick into the melted chocolate and then paint a scary face on your candy pumpkin. You can stick a toothpick through the pumpkin and tie a small piece of green yarn on top for a stem.

* Add some small cookies shaped like cats, wolves, or owls. You can also use small plastic spiders or other spooky creatures for decoration.

A Creepy Crossword Puzzle

Down:

1. Who is the birthday party for?
2. Which neighbor wants the Hauntlys to leave Dedman Street?
3. The Hauntlys' cat is named _____.

Across:

4. The Hauntly Manor Inn is what number on Dedman Street?
5. What color is Boris' cape?
6. Boris and Kilmer throw a _____ party.

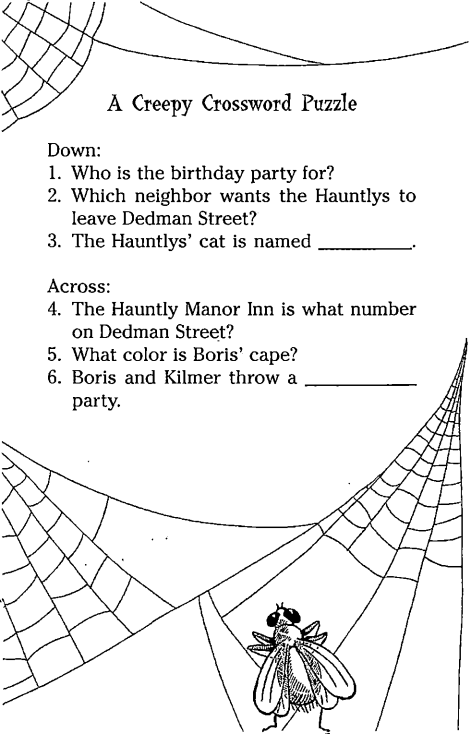

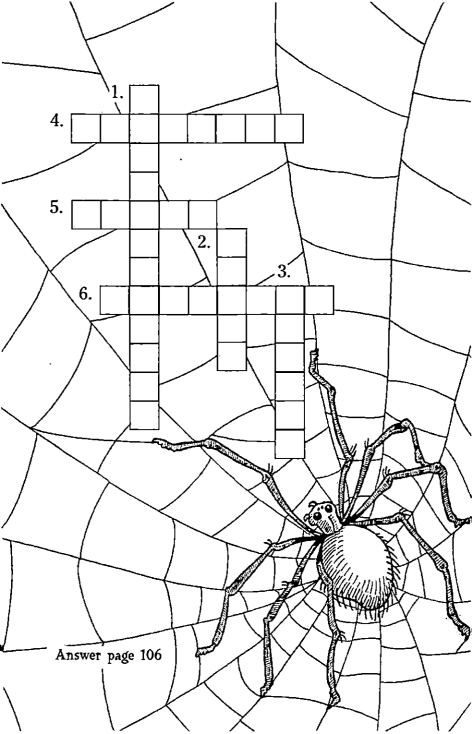

1.

4.

5.

2.

3.

6.

Answer page 106

Make Your Own Spooky Spider!

You will need:

2 paper plates
some black paint and a paintbrush
glue
8 black pipe cleaners
a pencil
a bottle cap
scissors
yellow paper
hole puncher
12-inch piece of white string

1. Paint the outside of the two paper plates black. Let dry completely.
2. Glue four pipe cleaners to the inside of one plate. Make sure that they are even. Glue the other four pipe cleaners on the opposite side of the plate.

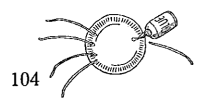

104

3. Glue the rim of the plate and place the second plate on top. Let dry.

4. Use a pencil to trace around the bottle cap to make two circles on the yellow paper. Carefully cut out the circles. Using your hole puncher, make two circles in the middle of the yellow circles. Glue these eyes on the top plate toward the edge of the plate.

5. Using your hole puncher, make a hole near the edge of the plate opposite from where you placed the eyes. Put the piece of string through the hole and make a knot. You can now hang your spooky spider!

Puzzle Answers

Haunted Word Search
Page 97

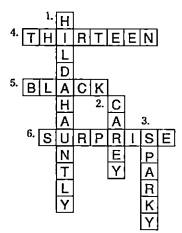

A Creepy Crossword Puzzle
Page 102

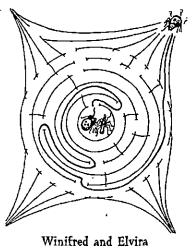

Winifred and Elvira
Maze Page 99

106